Through the Red Glass

S. P. Rowe

Duck 'n Row
11024 Balboa Blvd., #268, Granada Hills, CA 91344
info@ducknrow.com
Paperback ISBN: 979-8-9928411-3-8
Front cover art by Eli Tek
Interior design by Duck 'n Row
First Printing: 2025

To the 'better angels' of our nature.
May they prevail in daily battle—against the darkness
within.

DEPARTMENT OF THE ARMY
HEADQUARTERS, U.S, ARMY TEST AND EVALUATION COMMAND
Fort Hood, Texas

DATE: **FOR RECORD** 17 April 1972

FROM: Field Evaluation – AN/PVS-5 Night Observation
Goggles (Prototype)

1. Effective immediately, prototype equipment designated
'AN/PVS-5 Night Observation Goggles (Prototype' will be issued
to selected reconnaissance elements for operational
evaluation in field conditions.

2. Units: Issue L Company, 75th Infantry (RANGER) (LRRP),
10ist Airborne Division (Airmobile) – LRRP elements in
the A Shau/TA KO area.

3. Purpose: Conduct night reconnaissance, insertion/extraction
trials, and limited medevac drills to evaluate optical perfor-
mance under ███████████████████████████████
███████ Document malfunctions, tactical effectiveness for modi-
fication.

4. Location: TA KO (AMS Sheet 6440-1), A Shau corridor near
the Laos border, Approx. grid: ████████████

5. Reporting: After Action Reports (AARs) will be forwarded
to this headquarters via standard reporting chann-
nels, 'TEST DATA – FOR AUTHORIZED EVES ONLY'.

6. Security: Testing is RESTRICTED. Limit dissemination to
assigned units, MACV lialson officers, and ████████████.

FOR THE COMMANDER:
COL. JAMES R. HENDERSON
Test Director
Army Test and Evaluation
Command

DISTRIBUTION: LIMITED

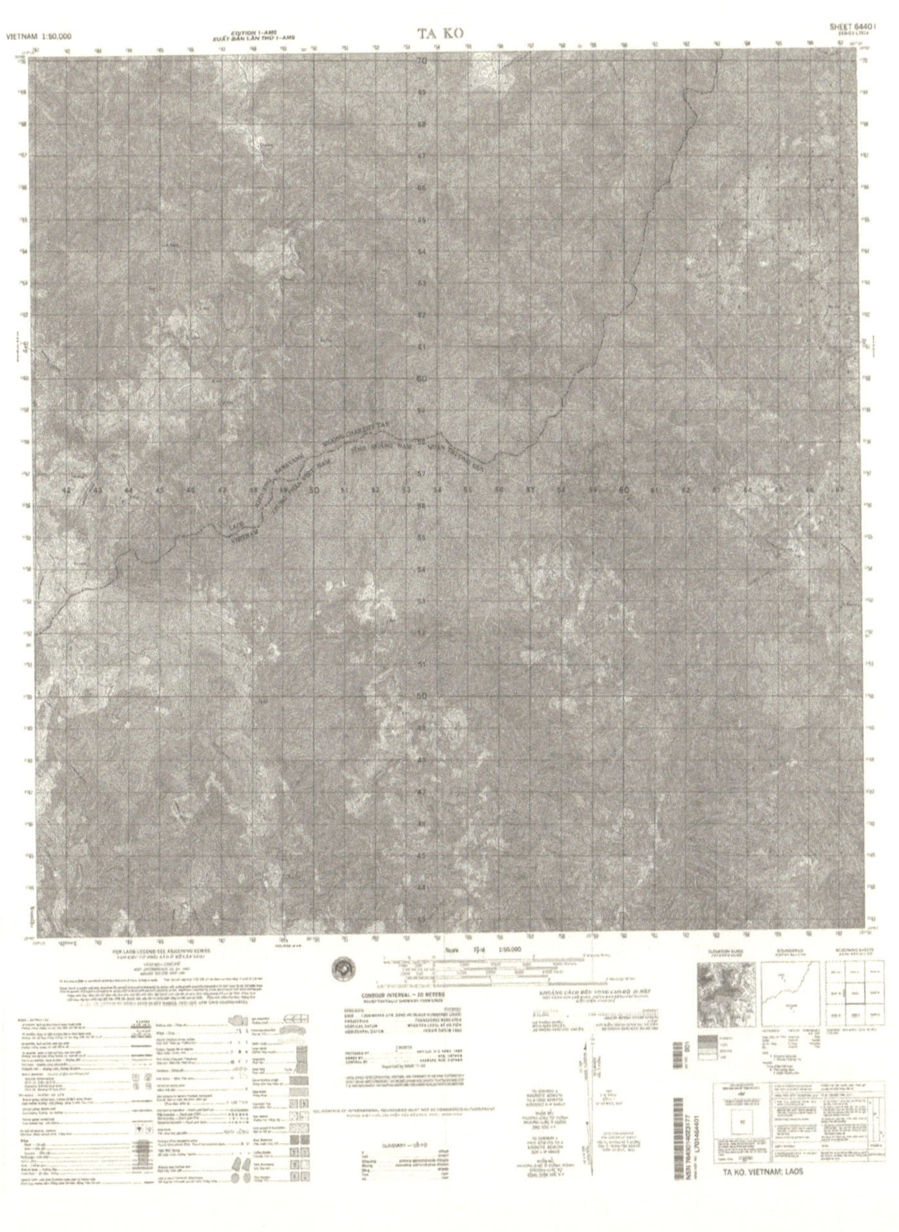

VIETNAM 1:50,000
EDITION 1-AMS
XUẤT BẢN LẦN THỨ 1-AMS
TA KO
SHEET 6440 I
SERIES L7014
TA KO, VIETNAM; LAOS
CONTOUR INTERVAL = 20 METERS
Scale 1:50,000
FOR LAOS LEGEND SEE ADJOINING KEYED
GLOSSARY — GÓ KO

Based on a true story.

Contents

Stuck

Sundown. Vietnam. 1972.

Under a crimson sky, at the edge of an ancient and dense jungle; two men pull a large metal barrel through a muddy field over rugged terrain. **It rains all the damn time in this country, at least it seems to.** Ruminates Sargent Garcia. He's been in the 'Nam since '69, though it feels he has spent an entire lifetime in this God forsaken hellhole. **I volunteered for this shit. Now I'm posted in the asshole of the universe.** Garcia, shakes his head. He's a large Latino man with a tight buzzcut that's 'all about its business'. His uniform, though well used and worn, is still kept in good clean order—even after all this time. Garcia's boots are shiny—before the rain anyway— and his shirt is well-pressed. Garcia's a crew chief with the recon group; setting a good example is part of the job: of course. As he drags the barrel forward through the muck, a bead-necklace reveals itself around his neck. The mud suctions against the bottom of the cylinder as the two men haul the barrel forward, making its relocation to the runway even more difficult. The other man, smaller and much younger, stops for a moment— catching his breath. Gasping, and with a look of exasperation on his face, he looks-up at Garcia on the other side of the barrel.

"Sarge!" he huffs. "It's stuck!"

Garcia looks-up with a stoic expression. "Sure is, Johnson."

This kid was probably buying Slurpees at the local 7-Eleven back in Michigan a month ago. Garcia huffs to himself. Shouldn't expect too much from the boy upfront. Garcia sighs as he braces his body against the barrel, trying to leverage his full weight against it. As he shoves the black cylinder forward, Johnson, with a look of guilt on his face, reaches for the barrel once again. As he does, the barrel rips loose from the mud, lurching forward unexpectedly. Johnson's hand, finding nothing but open air to keep his balance, is betrayed by its utter lack of support—his entire body follows to the ground, crashing into the juicy mud.

With a desperate cry that's both disgust and desperation, Johnson rolls onto his back. Now covered in mud from head to toe, he resembles a pig in a trough. With contempt for his current situation, Johnson wipes his face, trying to clear the filth from his eyes.

"This sucks."

Garcia laughs. "Sure does, Johnson."

He smiles for the first time and extends his hand, which Johnson gratefully accepts.

"Welcome to the suck."

Garcia pulls the boy back onto his feet in one swift motion.

"Gotta embrace that shit."

Johnson laughs as he clocks the ridiculousness of his situation. "Embrace the suck?"

"That's right." Garcia checks his watch. "No mas. Let's get these hellos fueled up, and then we'll get you cleaned up. Ok?"

"Thanks, Sarge."

With renewed vigor, the two men drag the fuel canister onto more solid ground; bringing the Landing Zone into view on the other side of a gently sloping hill. The trees had been blasted out for the aircraft a few days earlier, making room for reconnaissance operations further north. Can't kill Charlie if you can't find him, and that's the job of the LRRPs. The service members are ever mindful of their surroundings—Viet Cong are everywhere at night: in the rice paddies, in the jungle, in your goddamn cornflakes by the light of the moon. Find 'em. Kill 'em. Eat 'em up. That's the mission.

The sun's almost down now, and evil's on the menu. Always is—morning, noon, and night. Garcia thinks to himself as they drag the fuel barrel closer to the LZ. **But tonight, the Hueys eat first.**

As the two enlisted men pivot toward the runway, Johnson halts, "Sarge?"

Johnson's frozen in his tracks as a look of absolute terror washes over his face. Garcia notices that Johnson's eyes are fixed on the tree line.

"What is it, Johnson?"

Johnson's throat tightens as he tries to speak, but no words come—only a low moan escapes his lips as he raises his finger, pointing toward the jungle's edge. Hundreds of green eyes, glowing in the lush vegetation of the tree line, seem to stare back at them with all the hatred of hell made manifest.

Quietly, Johnson manages to choke through the words. "What. The fuck. Is that..?"

"Bioluminescent fungi," Garcia answers.

"What?"

"Bioluminescent fungi. They grow in the jungle. Glow in the dark."

Johnson's fear shifts into rage as he grips the fuel barrel once again. "Man. Fuck this place."

...

At the LZ, Sgt. Garcia flips through dirty damp paperwork as he signs over the fuel barrel to an anxious ground crew who impatiently await its contents. They're a little behind, but it shouldn't

4

delay mission start. To his left, Garcia hears the sound of falling water coming from a makeshift shower stall on the side of the runway. Hastily constructed among the old crates and refuse, it gets the job done. Besides, Johnson can't go to mission brief as he is. **Captain Stevens would rip us both new assholes.** Garcia mutters to himself.

Taking a rare moment to rest, Garcia walks over to one of the old wooden crates and leans against it. He listens to the sounds of the shower, focusing on the impact of every droplet as it hits the ground in relentless succession. Then, all at once, a memory floods back to him. He remembers floating at the bottom of that well. The well he jumped into, to evade enemy detection after a helicopter crash some years ago. Garcia remembers floating up to his neck, treading water in the darkness as droplets of rain relentlessly pelt his forehead from above. **How many days has it been? Three? Five?**

"All good now," Johnson reports. "Thanks Sarge!"

 Garcia flinches. He can't help but be a little started by Johnson.

"Good. Let's go."

Through the Red Glass

Four Huey helicopters in the makeshift LZ are fueled by ground crews as the reconnaissance team falls into line on the runway, Garcia's downright bored as he listens to their captain drone on about "body counts" and "victory." **Where do they manufacture these guys?** Garcia wonders. Captain Stevens sure fits 'the profile'. He's a tall man in his early thirties with a strong baritone voice that cuts through any battlefield noise. He's all about 'the mission'. **These West Point guys are always chasing medals.** Garcia rolls his eyes internally. The real victory, as far as Garcia's concerned, is watching the sunrise after a mission. To live another day. He's made a small tradition out of it, taking in the first light of the sun, post mission, with a beer in one hand and a rosary in the other.

Captain Stevens' lips curl into a smile as his eyes shift toward a crate at the edge of the muddy runway. "Now." He shifts topic. "I'm pleased to inform you that Christmas has come early this year." One of Stevens' lieutenants, as if on cue, flips open the crate with a long black crowbar, revealing the contents inside.

"Gentlemen. These are the AN/PVS-5 night vision goggles. They tell me it's a prototype. First of their kind, fresh off the line."

The lieutenant lifts one of the units from the crate and walks through its operation. Putting the goggles on his head, he pulls the system over his eyes. Two giant lenses, similar to an owl's eyes, peer darkly toward the recon platoon. Then the Lt. flips a switch on the left side of the helmet. The two black lenses illuminate with a bright red light as the soldier turns his head back and forth.

"Starlight. Moonlight. The lens have a special Dicyanin coating, and the state-of-the-art optics are amplified for sight in the night. Our job is to test these 'night vision' goggles in an operational situation."

"Can't kill Charlie if you can't find him." Garcia says softly.

Overhearing Garcia, Capt. Stevens smirks, "Can't kill Charlie if you can't SEE him."

Garcia hears the energetic sound of engines firing up as the red-light goggles are distributed to the unit. The familiar chop of propeller blades slice through the air with increasing speed, as the vibrations echo from the trees.

"Let's take back the night. Mount up!"

...

The helicopter crews fall-out-of-line and jog to their respective Huey's on the runway. Johnson turns toward Garcia with a juvenile smirk as he pulls an M60 machine gun from a nearby crate.

"Loading up, Sgt," Beams Johnson as he cracks open the bullet chamber.

Garcia nods as he steps onto the skid tubes of his helicopter. Without conscience intention, he finds his fingers gripping the bead necklace around his neck. As Johnson fumbles with the 7.62 belts, Garcia pulls the necklace from under his fatigue shirt revealing a rosary cross. He prays quietly, for himself, for the group:

"Hail Mary, full of grace, pray for us sinners, now and at the hour of our death. Amen."

He was lucky to be alive they said. Capt. Stevens told Garcia, that this far north the jungle craws with VC activity—as if Garcia didn't have direct experience with Charlie himself. They told Garcia he'd been floating in the well for ten days in total, when the search team found and pulled him out. In the end, he didn't even have the stars to keep him company—thanks to the endless rain of these cursed monsoons.

Still, he never felt alone.

Johnson interrupts Garcia's mediations once again, "Locked and loaded, Sarge."

"That's fine, Johnson. Well done."

...

Army reconnaissance patrol. Condition green.

Four recon helicopters, flying in a single-file 'trail formation' cut northward now, through the twilight sky. Garcia sits in the interior of the Huey, behind the pilot cabin; facing the tail of the aircraft. He grips the ridged surface of the handhold by his seat as he listens to the radio blasting over the oppressive noise of the rotor blades above them. Opposite his position sits Johnson inside a cubbyhole by the door. He nervously scans the jungle below as they sail over the tree-tops and through the sky. As the door gunner, his M60 is trained on a sea of branches blowing past—a deep maze of foliage whose depths, and threats, remain unknown.

The kid hasn't been in country long. Garcia reflects. **But he's a good shot. He'll be ok.**

"Alright, gentlemen! Let's go to V-formation."

His thoughts are interrupted by Capt. Stevens' booming voice as he sends out orders to the other Hueys.

The pilot sitting next to Capt. Stevens responds, "Roger. V-formation."

The other helicopters comply with nimble precision, moving out of 'trail' and crossing into 'V-formation'. It's a strong formation, good for mutual support and quick peel-off flank attacks. Designed for ass-kicking—amen.

"Tighten up! Alright. Seems calm enough," Capt. Stevens mutters as the last light fades over the horizon. "Gunners. Ready to play with the new gear?"

"Yes sir."

Through the intercom headset, Garcia hears the door gunners check-in from the other Hueys in the recon group. Then, he hears Johnson's voice.

"Sir."

Capt. Stevens is almost giddy, "Ho! Ho! Ho! That's a go for goggles. Go goggles."

Garcia watches Johnson pull the AN/PVS-5 night vision goggles down from his forehead. The large, round lenses illuminate with an eerie red light as Johnson flips the switch on the left-hand side.

"Wow!"

Johnson pans his head back and forth, as if seeing a new world for the first time.

"This is nuts," reports another door gunner over the intercom from 'Huey Two'.

Garcia can feel Capt. Stevens smiling from here as he jumps back into the conversation. "Is it working?"

"Sir. Yes sir," Johnson answers quickly. "It's all red. But I can see everything!"

"Outstanding!" replies Stevens. "How's the detail?"

"Can see the treetops, clearly, sir. I—"

Johnson pauses. His head stops scanning, focusing in on something low to the horizon.

His body tenses. He screams as he opens fire with his M60 machine gun.

BRAP! BRAAAAAAAP!

Green tracer rounds rip through the sky in a colorful and deadly display as Johnson lays down a barrage of 7.62mm bullets at eleven shots per second.

Garcia hears their helicopter pilot over the radio, "Condition red. Condition red."

From the passenger seat, Capt. Stevens turns his head, looking over his shoulder toward the back of the cabin.

He barks at Johnson, "What do you see, son?!"

Garcia looks in the direction of the gunfire, but sees no one. No enemy. No vehicles. Nothing.

Johnson screams again. "My god!"

BRAAAAAAAP!

Capt. Stevens' voice cuts sternly over the intercom.

"Cease fire."

"Cease fire."

But, Johnson doesn't stop. He screams even louder as his firing rate increases. The tracer rounds streak dangerously close to another Huey attack helicopter in formation on their left.

Garcia hears their pilot behind him call out the imminent threat over the radio. "Two. Two. Friendly fire. Watch your three. Pull up! Pull up!"

BRAAAAAAAAAAAAAP!

Johnson mashes down his trigger completely. No longer firing in bursts, he sprays more rounds into the sky. As Huey Two tries to pull up and out of the firing path, several tracers slam into the skid tubes below the helicopter—a near-deadly hit.

That's enough. Garcia leaps up from his seat, and charges across the open cabin. Reaching Johnson, he grabs onto him, boxing out the flashing muzzle of the M60 with his body.

"Cease fire! Goddamnit!" Garcia shouts as he slams his body into Johnson's. Pinning him to the wall, Garcia pulls the weapon from Johnson's tight grip. In terror, Johnson rips the goggles from his face, his two horrified eyes are almost as wide as the lenses themselves.

"Demons!" Johnson exclaims.

"What?!!" Garcia snaps, securing the weapon.

"There are fucking demons flying around out there! Oh Jesus! Oh god!"

"What the fuck is going on back there, Sergeant?!!!" shouts Capt. Stevens.

"I don't know, sir!" answers Garcia. "Weapon secured."

Chapter 3

Deliver Us from Evil

The captain calls a mission abort, the recon team is returning to base. Sitting on the edge of the chopper, Garcia watches the ground grow closer as they descend to the landing zone. **This mission can't end fast enough**, he laments. He looks over to Johnson, who's bracing in the corner. He hasn't stopped praying since the incident:

"Deliver us from evil."
"Deliver us from evil."
"Deliver us from evil."

Johnson began the Lord's Prayer some time ago, but when he arrived at that phrase he locked into it, repeating the words over and over, begging for protection from invisible forces.

Touchdown.

Stevens looks back at Garcia, who quietly nods. "I've got him, sir."

Captain Stevens replies with a note of compassion in his voice as he heads towards the barracks.

"Debrief in twenty."

"Yes, sir," Garcia answers.

"Hey! HEY!" a man shouts from across the LZ.

Garcia turns toward the angry voice. It's the crew of 'Huey Two', the four men are understandably furious, and heading his way.

"What the fuck, Garcia!" says the pilot of Huey Two.

"That's close enough," Garcia warns as the pilot trudges toward Johnson. "Sir. Lt. Stop."

The pilot, wild-eyed with rage, takes a swing at Garcia, who sidesteps and counters with an uppercut to the pilots face. The pilot falls backward into the mud, nursing a bloody nose. Garcia opens his arms toward the other men in a gesture of truce.

"No mas," he says quietly.

The pilot, still sitting in the mud, complains to himself. His tone has shifted from rage to frustration. "What happened out there, man?"

"I'm going to find out. You have my word."

The crew of 'Huey Two' pick-up their pilot and head toward the barracks after Capt. Stevens, who is now some distance away from the runway. Garcia's own pilot collects Johnson from the cubby hole. As they pass Garcia, Johnson runs-up to him, dropping his red-light goggles into the mud.

"Demons, man! I saw them!" Johnson pleads desperately. "I'm not crazy. You gotta believe me, man!"

Garcia responds quietly, "Get cleaned up, Johnson. I got your six."

In relief, tears stream down Johnson's face—someone might actually believe him about tonight. As Garcia watches his crew trudge back toward the barracks, he notices the red-light goggles sticking out of the mud. After a moment of hesitation, Garcia reaches down and tugs them free.

...

He walks away from the LZ, and into the darkness before the dawn. He heads toward the barbed wire marking the outer boundary of the base. Standing there, at the edge of the dark jungle, Garcia puts the goggles on top of his head. With a labored sigh, he pulls the large round lenses over his eyes.

"Fuck it." He growls, flipping the power switch on the left-hand side of the AN/PVS-5.

He hears the whir of the headset powering up. At that moment, the edge of the forest transforms from an indistinguishable black pitch to a brilliant red landscape. Every branch, every shrub visible now, through the red glass.

Then he sees it. Hanging upside down, directly across from him on the nearest tree, is a human-like figure. But it's not human, nor does it have skin. The reddish monster of sinew and bone resembles a giant bat. Giant wings stretch out from its torso as it hangs upside down from a branch, eyes closed, apparently sleeping. Garcia's adrenaline surges as he rips the goggles up from of his eyes—but he sees nothing.

The branch is empty.

He studies the goggles with suspicion.

"What are these things!" Garcia growls to himself.

Pulling the lenses over his eyes for a second time, he zooms-in on the same branch. The monster's there once again, hanging from the tree. Now with open eyes, it marks Garcia with glowing green cat-like pupils, fixing on him with an unholy gaze. Before Garcia can react, the creature outstretches into its full wingspan and smiles.

It's a cruel smile, with razor teeth, and long fangs. The grin of a demon embracing war and death, reveling in its hatred of all creation.

It's the smile though, that makes Garcia's blood run cold. Such a familiar look on such an unnatural face. Then, in a moment of recognition, he releases that he's see this exact look before—at the bottom of the well.

He remembers running for his life as the enemy Kong chased him. How he reached a small abandoned village in a jungle clearing with a well in the center. He remembers thinking that the old sparse buildings are a terrible hiding place, as the enemy will search them. He recalls clumsily dropping his survival pistol and vaulting over the side of the old cobblestone well, and into the shaft below. He remembers falling for some time and then crashing through the surface of the water at the bottom of the well. Garcia meditates on the memory of the cold slowly soaking into his uniform as he floats in the darkness.

Did they see me? Garcia remembers thinking, as he looks skyward through the circular cobblestones toward the surface. He remembers hearing the Viet Kong quietly searching the buildings in the square. He recollects trying to control his breathing, in fear that the slightest exhale, or pater in the water, would give away his position.

Then, at the top of the well, a figure emerges. It's a Vietnamese boy no older than fifteen, clad in black pajamas. The boy peers over the edge with an old Chinese SKS battle rifle trained downward into the darkness. Garcia remembers a sensation of instant terror as the two make eye contact over the target sights of the boy's weapon. The stark contrast of an innocent looking face against the black death of a pointed barrel, threatening to kill him any moment.

Garcia remembers raising his arms above the water in a gesture of--surrender? An appeal to their common humanity? **Please don't shoot me.** He remembers thinking. He recalls being able to breathe again as the boy lowers his service rifle, and the rush of relief over his body--that he may yet, survive. He also remembers the feeling of horror return, as the boy with innocent face's eyes turn dark. He helplessly looks-on as the

boy's expression transforms into a smile of pure
hatred. It's the smile Garcia is seeing now, at the
jungle's edge: the smile of a demon.

The boy is toying with him, as Garcia floats
helplessly at the bottom of the well. He waves
mockingly at Garcia, with a grenade in his hand.
Garcia remembers the metallic sound of the pin
being removed from the safety catch:

Ching!

Most of all, Garcia recalls the boy's hateful smirk
as the live grenade falls toward him.

He remembers taking the deepest breath he has
ever taken. Filling his lungs almost to bursting as
he dives down under water. Furiously kicking his
legs, he swims downward as the grenade explodes
over head. By the time he realizes that he's still
alive, bullets trail through the water at high
speed, slicing through the liquid in swift and
deadly bubble trails.

There, under the water, Garcia curls into a fetal
position. Praying. Waiting at the crossroads for
the next moment for his life--or death--to be
decided.

As long as he can, Garcia holds his breath. Until
his face turns red and his blood screams. Still he
waits, suspended in the chilly water at the bottom
of the well. He waits until he can't wait any longer.
He waits until his lungs demand payment and will
have water or air, they care not which.

This is it. Garcia muses. Bursting through the surface of the water, Garcia expects to be met with bullets. But, there's no one at the top. The boy is gone. **He must have thought I was dead. Or did he care enough to check, at all?**

Then back in the LZ, at the jungle's edge on the other side of the world; this demonic encounter-- ends. A bright light cuts through the lenses, blinding Garcia. He flips the goggles up, and off. The demon is gone. Dawn breaks through the trees, banishing the evil in the first rays of a rising sun.

Or perhaps this evil is always here? Invisible to man's sight?

Are they watching?

Influencing?

Making us hate each other?

Pssssscct.

Garcia pulls a beer from his side pocket, opens it, chugs it down, and tosses the can aside. He pulls-out a rosary, the beaded-necklace, from under his fatigue shirt.

"Hail Mary, full of grace, pray for us sinners, now and at the hour of our death. Amen."

Finishing the prayer, Garcia drops the red-light goggles into the mud. He violently stomps on them, grinding them into the mud with the heal of his boot. Without another thought, he turns back toward the barracks.

As he walks, Garcia feels the warmth of the rising sun on his back and the triumph of seeing the sunrise, once again.

THE END

Epilogue

Dawn. Oxford. 1911.

A man stands in the center of a circular room. It's a dark, brooding lecture hall, of the academic variety with mahogany stadium seating ascending upward from the bottom level. On a regular day this would give the attendees in the stands of a 'packed house' the best possible view of the speaker on the ground level, below.

Today, however, the room hasn't reached even a third of it's capacity as the man in the center of the lecture hall delivers a nervous recitation from his own book.

"The Human Atmosphere"

"By Walter John Kilner. Myself."

Looking upward into an indifferent crowd, a small gaunt man named Walter Kilner returns his eyes to the pages of chapter one. Having spent a lifetime indoors his dark brown hair marks a sharp contrast to his pale white complexion. A complexion that's possibly paler than the pages of the book he's reading from.

He continues, "Hardly one person in ten thousand is aware that he or she is surrounded by a haze intimately connected with the body, whether asleep or awake, whether hot or cold, which, although invisible under ordinary circumstances, can be seen when conditions are favourable."

"Auras? Poppycock!" Shouts a man from the dark seating area.

Kilner raises his hand in protest, "Gentlemen please. We'll have questions after the reading."

The small academic crowd of both students and professors grumbles quietly. Somewhere between rudeness and outright interruption, Kilner hazards back into the pages of his book.

Attempting to preserve his dignity with a stern, if not shaky, tone of voice, he finds his place again in the first paragraph of chapter one, "This mist, the prototype of the halo or nimbus constantly depicted around the saints, has been manifested to certain individuals possessing a specially gifted sight—"

"Psydo-science!" Another man shouts from above.

Kilner maintains his stern tone, slightly raising his voice over this latest interruption as he attempts to 'win back' the room, "who have received the title of "Clairvoyants," and until quite recently, to no one else. It may as well be stated at once that we make not the slightest claim to clairvoyancy; nor are we occultists—"

"But, that is what you are!" An old tenured professor leaps to his feet in a huff. His 'burnside' beard seems to defy gravity, almost parting from his checks on the bounce. But, the beard holds fast to him, though, as he steps forward in a blur of shaggy accusation. "You sir, are an Occultist! I'm leaving, and I dare say that no serious 'man of science', who values his name-sake or reputation—will hear another word."

Kilner makes an appeal, "Doctor? Please."

The old professor raises his hand, 'enough'. He limps slowly toward the exit on an old cane as the rest of the faculty rises to their feet. Kilner's eyes widen as his worst nightmare is realized, after years of research, painstaking 'trial and error', and disappointing failures—the faculty of Oxford are walking out on him.

"Gentleman, please!" Kilner gasps, "There's so much more to share."

Kilner looks about the room, realizing that soon—if nothing changes—he'll be speaking to a hall of empty chairs. He'd intended to keep his invention a surprise. A grand finale! Alas. Kilner wanted to win these men over with his sharp prose and exhaustive research. He wanted to open, at least a small crack, in the 'close-mindedness' and supposed 'rationality' of modern academia. He sees now, that they require more than mere theory.

As the remaining attendees of the lecture head for the exits. Kilner jogs to a table in the center of the floor. Hastily, he rakes for the metal locks of his briefcase. The locks flip open with an awkward click as Kilner wastes no more time. He pulls open the black case and grabs a leather object from the pouch inside.

Lifting the object high above his head, Kilner shows-off his invention to the remaining academics.

"I say! That, the Aura can be made visible by the aid of chemical screens!"

Silence grips the room.

Then, audible gasps echo from the rafters as Kilner places a pair of leather goggles onto his forehead. The unmistakable circular red lenses adorn the center as Kilner glares at the remaining crowd with a mix of triumph and arrogance on his face.

Kilner studies the men, awaiting a reaction. Any reaction. Surely academia can't ignore 'applied science' in the field! The audience watches him, frozen-in-place where they stand, as Kilner pulls the goggles over his eyes.

Then it happens. A reaction emerges from the blank faces of these hardened academics of Oxford University. Their stern puritanical expressions turn upward into something Kilner doesn't expect: cruel smiles, accompanied by an even more hideous and unwelcome sound...

That of Laughter. Of ridicule.

The entire hall reverberates with the sound of scorn and rejection as Kilner stands dumbfounded, in the center of the room. Thanks to the room's nearly perfect acoustics in the lecture hall, Kilner is at once struck with wave after wave of derision. He freezes as this hostile laughter fills his ears.

Then, after what seems an eternity, the mercy of silence returns to the hall as the last academic exits the room. Kilner is alone again. Standing at the center of the empty lecture hall with only his book and goggles to keep him company. With despair, Kilner removes the red goggles from his face and crosses back behind the desk to collect his things.

Angrily tossing his equipment and papers into his briefcase, Kilner prepares to make his escape once again from academia. From the straight-jacket of reason. He'll try somewhere else. There must be someone willing to listen!

Suddenly, Kilner hears a voice. The strong baritone timbre cuts through the silence of the air like a trumpet.

"Mr. Walter Kilner."

"What now!" Kilner snaps back.

Kilner steadies himself. He can't believe that he's allowed the ugliness of the previous moment to affect him so. Kilner takes a deep breath, calming his nerves, as he peers into the darkly lit stadium seating.

"My deepest apologies. I thought everyone had left."

The voice replies, "That so? I've come a long way to be here today, Mr. Kilner. If you wouldn't mind continuing? I'd sure appreciate it."

Excitement surges from within Kilner, finally, someone's listening! Someone may understand the true potential of his discovery!

"Of course!" Kilner restrains himself, returning to a more academic demeanor,

"Of course, sir."

He re-opens his briefcase once again, and then once again sets it's contents meticulously on the table at the bottom of the lecture hall. There's an awkward silence. Kilner realizes that he's being a little rude, once more he peers into the darkness with an inquisitive expression, "Ready. Umm. Who might I be addressing? Sir?"

The man in the darkness leans forward into the light. He's a tall man, in his early thirties. The American wears the olive military uniform of a 'dough boy.'

"Capt. Stevens. United States Army," The ageless man smiles from under his hat.

"Please proceed, sir."

DEPARTMENT OF THE ARMY TECHNICAL MANUAL

HAND RECEIPT MANUAL
COVERING END ITEM/COMPONENTS OF END ITEM (COEI), BASIC ISSUE ITEMS (BII), AND ADDITIONAL AUTHORIZATION LIST (AAL)
FOR
NIGHT VISION GOGGLES AN/PVS-5 AND AN/PVS-5A
(NSN 5855-00-150-1820)
LINE ITEM NUMBER N04456

Headquarters, Department of the Army, Washington, DC
21 July 1979

Current as of 26 February 1979

REPORTING ERRORS AND RECOMMENDING IMPROVEMENTS
You can help improve this manual by calling attention to errors and by recommending improvements and stating your reasons for the recommendations. Your letter or DA Form 2028 (Recommended Changes to Publications and Blank Forms) should be mailed direct to Commander, US Army Communications and Electronics Materiel Readiness Command, ATTN: DRSEL-ME-MQ, Fort Monmouth, New Jersey 07703. A reply will be furnished direct to you.

Table of Contents

Section I INTRODUCTION

1. Scope

This Hand Receipt Manual provides a listing on a preprinted DA Form 2062 (Hand Receipt) of accountable End Items/COEI, BII, and AAL items related to Night Vision Goggles AN/PVS 5 and AN/PVS 5.A.

2. General

Section II of this manual is an overprinted DA Form 2062 consisting of a listing of The End Item/Components of End Items (COEI), Basic Issue Items (BII), and Additional Authorization List (AAL) items extracted from TM 11-5855-238-10. The listings consist of exactly the same items and are in the same sequence as the End Item/COEI, BII, and AAL listings in the operator's manual. The overprinted DA Form 2062 will aid property accountability officers in preparation of hand receipts referred by AR 710 2. Local reproduction of the overprinted DA Form 2062 is authorized. Additional copies of the HR manual may be requisitioned from the US Army Army Adjutant General Publications Center, 1655 Woodson Road, St. Louis, MO 63114, in accordance with Chapter 3, AR 310-2.

3. Explanation of Blocks and Columns

a. *FROM.* Enter the organization for which the property book is maintained.

b. *TO.* Enter the (UIC) and the hand receipt file number of the unit/ personnel receiving the property.

c. *CATALOG NO.* Contains the technical manual (TM) number of the operator's manual

d. *CURR OF ALW.* Not applicable.

e. *ITEM.* Contains end item short title

f. *STOCK NO.* National stock number of the item described.

g. *ITEM DESCRIPTION.* Identifies the item contained in the COEI, BII, and AAL. Contains nomenclature, and serial/USA number (if applica ble) that will be useful in identifying and controlling the item. Serial number to be inserted and initialed **on** all copies by the hand receipt holder.

h. T (a). Quantity of each item as listed in the COEI, BII, and AAL.

i. C (t). Leave blank.

j. BALANCE.

(1) *1.* Enter the total quantity possessed by the receiving unit/personnel for each item listed. All quantity totals will be advanced to the next balance column on any item changes, annotated "adjusted," dated, and signed by the individual receiving the property.

(2) *2.* The individual receiving property will sign and date the appropriate balance column on the bottom of the last page below a drawn line. When an inventory is taken, the column will be annotated "Per inventory."

(3). *3* through *12.* Same as (2) above.

k. PAGE NO/NO. OF PAGES. Contains page number and total pages for the COEI, BII, and AAL portions of the hand receipt. Hand receipt holders initial each page no. (only when two or more forms are involved). When hand receipt holders change, the old initials will be lined out and new hand receipt holder will initial each page.

Section II HAND RECEIPT

Following is hand receipt for Night Vision Goggles AN/PVS-5 or AN/PVS-5A.

HAND RECEIPT/ANNEX NO. For use of this form, see AR 710-2; the proponent agency is the office of the Deputy Chief of Staff for Logistics.		FROM:	TO: Hand Receipt File No.												
Following last item, state in each balance column the type of action *(e.g. issue, turn-in, inventory, etc.)* producing this balance, date of action, and signature.		Fill in the following when this form is used as Hand Receipt Annex.													
		CATALOG NO TM 11-5855-238-10	CURR OF ALW	ITEM AN/PVS-5 OR AN/PVS-5A											

STOCK NO	END ITEM/COMPONENTS OF END ITEM (COEI) ITEM DESCRIPTION	T (a)	C (t)	BALANCE											
				1	2	3	4	5	6	7	8	9	10	11	12
5855-00-125-0401	ADAPTER ASSEMBLY, ARCTIC	1													
5855-00-125-0713	HEADSTRAP ASSEMBLY	1													
7610-00-137-9197	SHEET, INSTRUCTION	1													
5855-00-125-0770	VEE STRAP ASSEMBLY	1													
5855-00-125-0403	DEMISTING SHIELD ASSEMBLY	1													
5120-00-044-2391	KEY, SOCKET HEAD	1													
6640-00-240-5851	LENS TISSUE	1													
	BASIC ISSUE ITEMS														
5855-00-138-2317	CASE ASSEMBLY, CARRYING	1													
5855-00-137-7768	CASE ASSEMBLY, SHIPPING AND STORAGE	1													
5340-00-132-4227	CAP, LENS, EYEPIECE	1													
5340-00-132-4264	CAP, LENS, OBJECTIVE	1													
	ADDITIONAL AUTHORIZATION LIST														
5855-00-125-0762	STRAP ASSEMBLY, AVIONICS	1													
5325-00-285-6295	FASTENER, SNAP STYLE 2	2													

T - Total allowance for Hand Receipts. (a) Authorized per item for Hand Receipt Annexes.
C - Current operating allowance for Hand Receipts. (t) Total authorized for Hand Receipt Annexes.

PAGE NO 1
NO. OF PAGES 2

DA FORM 2062 (1 JAN 58)

CURRENT AS OF 21 JULY 1979

ACKNOWLEDGMENTS

T his novella is my attempt to do something 'spooky'

for halloween.
I wanted to take an urban legend about Vietnam and 'run
with it'. What if
other entities exist beyond what our eyes and ears can
detect? What if they're influencing humanity constantly
without our knowledge or understanding?

My thanks to the wonderful cover artist, Eli Tek. Who nailed
the atmosphere and tone of the story in his artwork from
the very beginning.

I'd also like to thank Sabrina Kimball of Triple Moon
Proofing for her delightful feedback, and for proofing this
book with both the speed and charm that was quite
magical, indeed.

AUTHOR BIO

Sean is a writer and editor whose career bridges film, television, and fiction. A native of Baltimore now based in Los Angeles, he draws on his background in visual storytelling to craft narratives that are both cinematic and deeply human.

His work has appeared in the graphic novel anthology *321: Fast Comics*, and his wide-ranging interests—from military history to speculative science fiction—inform the scope and texture of his writing. Rowe's debut novel, *Under the Horn of Hearth*, launches the *Northland Frail* saga, a fantasy epic more than a decade in the making. His latest work, the novella *Through the Red Glass*, further demonstrates his fascination with myth-making, history, and the power of stories.